TO
AVERY + ELLIE

HAPPY
EASTER

Love
NANA 4-22

THE EASTER BUNNY
is coming to
INDIANA

Written by Eric James   Illustrated by Mari Lobo

sourcebooks
wonderland

The sweet Easter Bunny
is skipping along
through Indiana
singing this song:

Cakes

NOBLESVILLE
BOOKS

TINY THE
Indiana
EASTER BUNNY

The Littlest
Bunny in
Indiana

"The eggs are delivered.
My Easter job's done.
And now it is time
that I joined in the fun!"

She jumps down a tunnel
that runs underground,
and pops up again
in each city and town.

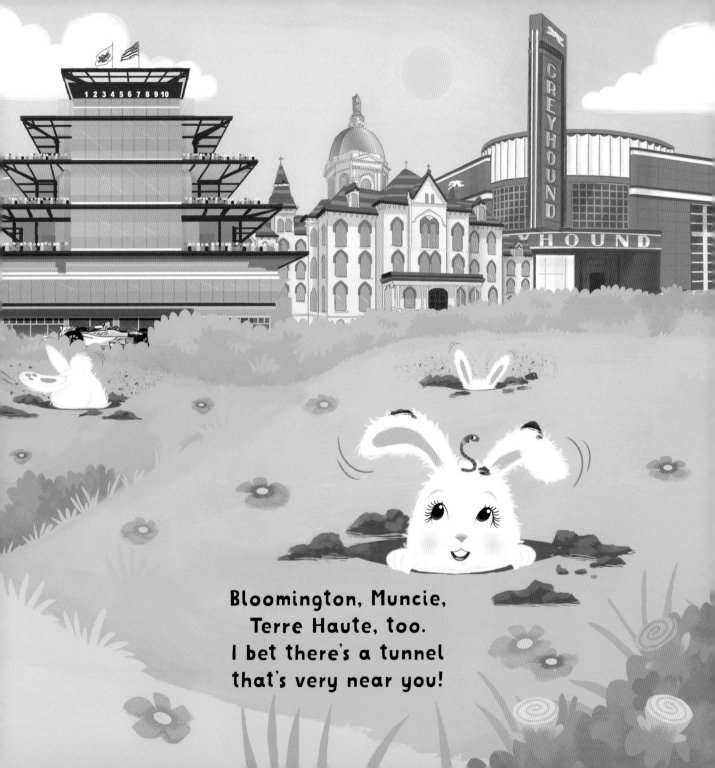

Bloomington, Muncie,
Terre Haute, too.
I bet there's a tunnel
that's very near you!

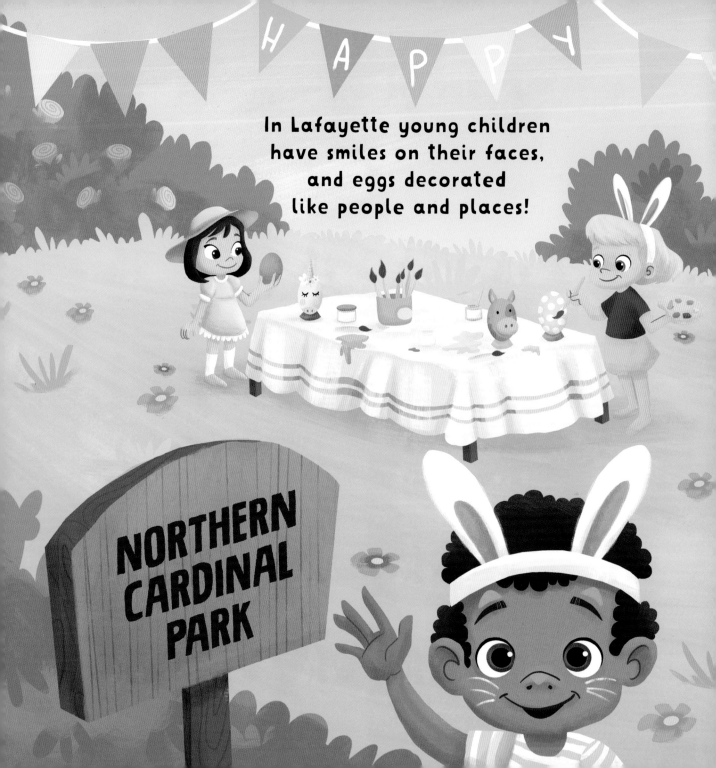

In Lafayette young children
have smiles on their faces,
and eggs decorated
like people and places!

NORTHERN
CARDINAL
PARK

But one little boy
drops the egg from his hands.
A loud **CRACKING** sound
can be heard as it lands.

"Oh dear!" says the bunny,
and dabs at a tear.
"You need cheering up
so thank goodness I'm here!"

She wiggles her ears,
she hops on the spot,
she waggles her tail,
and he giggles a lot!

In Indianapolis, there's
an Easter parade.
Most children are clapping
but one looks afraid.

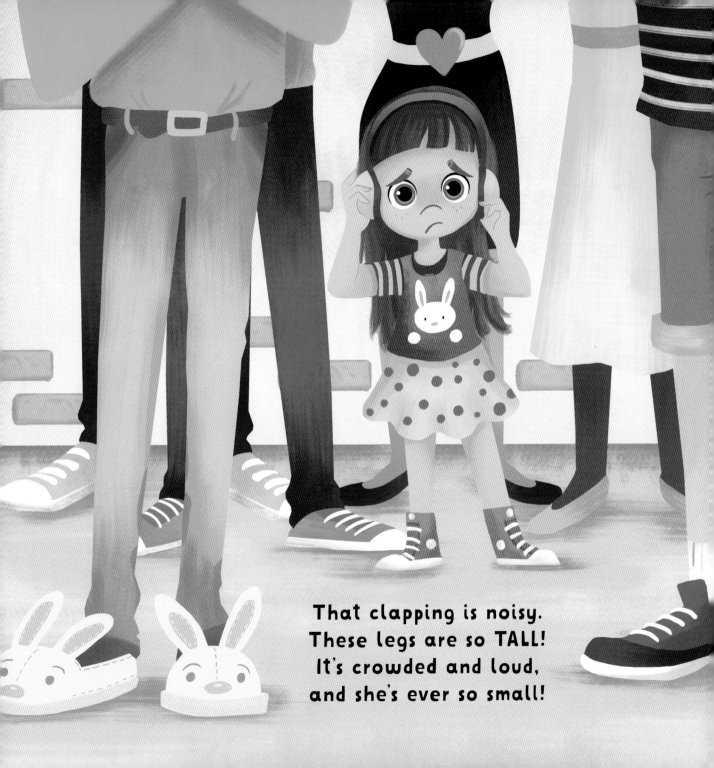

That clapping is noisy.
These legs are so TALL!
It's crowded and loud,
and she's ever so small!

"Gee whiz, what a din!
I know just what to do.
Come here little one
and I'll hold hands with you!"

She wiggles her ears,
and spins her around.
The little girl laughs
as her feet leave the ground!

Down in Fort Wayne
while having a rest,
the bunny eats Sugar Cream Pie.
(It's the best!)

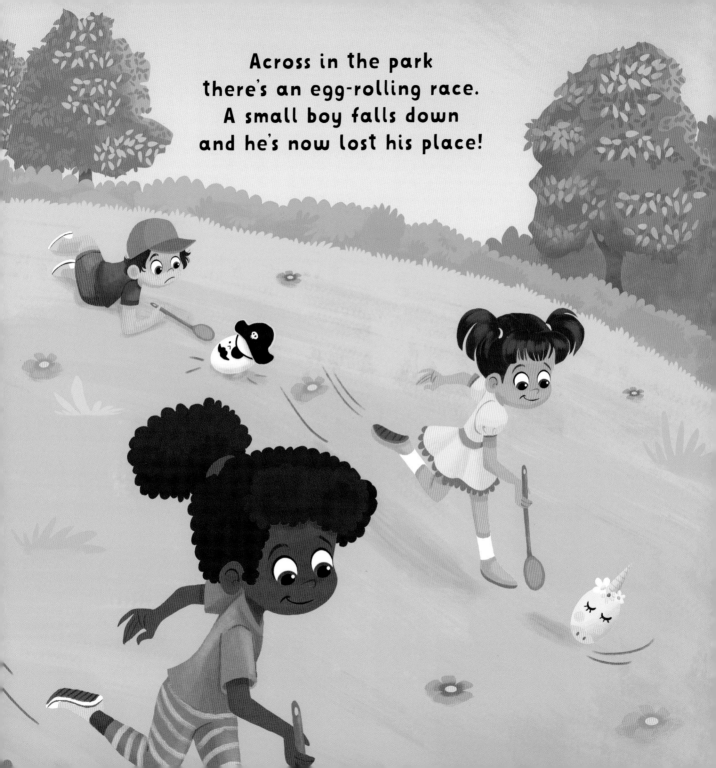

Across in the park
there's an egg-rolling race.
A small boy falls down
and he's now lost his place!

She's just a big blur
as she tumbles on past.
The boy runs to help her.
He's going so FAST!

FINISH

She wiggles her ears,
he can't (but he tries!).
They hop up and down
for they've just won first prize!

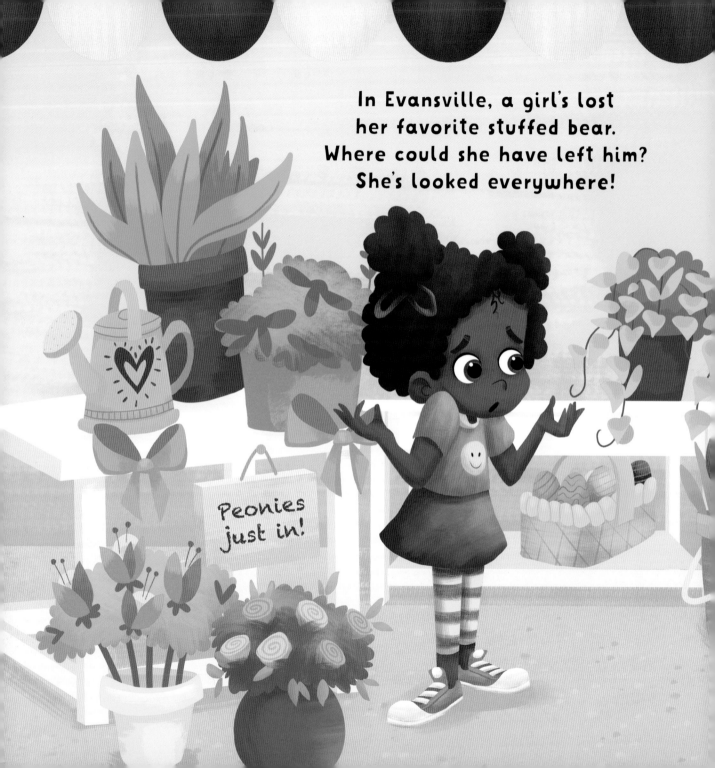

In Evansville, a girl's lost her favorite stuffed bear. Where could she have left him? She's looked everywhere!

Peonies just in!

"When I'm feeling sad
do you know what I do?
I hop up and down!
Do you want to try too?"

She wiggles her ears, the girl thinks it's funny,
and laughs even more when she hops like a bunny!

They both jump around like they haven't a care.
And look what the chicks have just found, over there!

In South Bend, the bunny
helps children with SHARING.

In Carmel, she helps a sweet child
to be DARING.

In French Lick she SINGS,
in Greencastle she WIGGLES.

Wherever she goes
she brings LAUGHTER and GIGGLES!

This day's been so busy
but also such fun.
The bunny daydreams
in the warm setting sun.

The twilight is coming,
the three chicks are lazing,
and tweeting about
how this day's been #AMAZING!

The bunny jumps up,
snapping out of her daze,
"There's only three-hundred-
and-sixty-four days!"

More chocolate needs making!
New eggs will need wrapping!
It's all so exciting,
the three chicks start flapping!

"Indiana is great
and we love being here.
We'll make lots more eggs
and we'll be back
next year!"

She wrinkles her nose,
she wiggles her ears,
she blows you a kiss,
and she just...disappears!

Written by Eric James
Illustrated by Mari Lobo
Additional artwork by Philip McIvor
Designed by Nicky Scott

Published by Sourcebooks Wonderland,
an imprint of Sourcebooks Kids
P.O. Box 4410, Naperville, Illinois 60567-4410
(630) 961-3900
sourcebookskids.com

Date of Production: October 2020
Run Number: 5019995
Printed and bound in China (1010)
10 9 8 7 6 5 4 3 2